Mail Monks

Written By

Rhonda Gowler Greene

Illustrated By

Robert Bender

Childcraft Education Corp.

To my dear father — a mailman
who never missed a day of work in
30 years.
— The Publisher

Childcraft Education Corp.
1156 Four Star Drive
Mount Joy, PA 17552

A member of the School Specialty® Family
Printed in China
ISBN 1-58669-217-8

In rain, sleet, or snow,
in heat, wind, or hail,
monkeys delight
in delivering mail.

A far destination?
They know what to do.
Their motto is always—

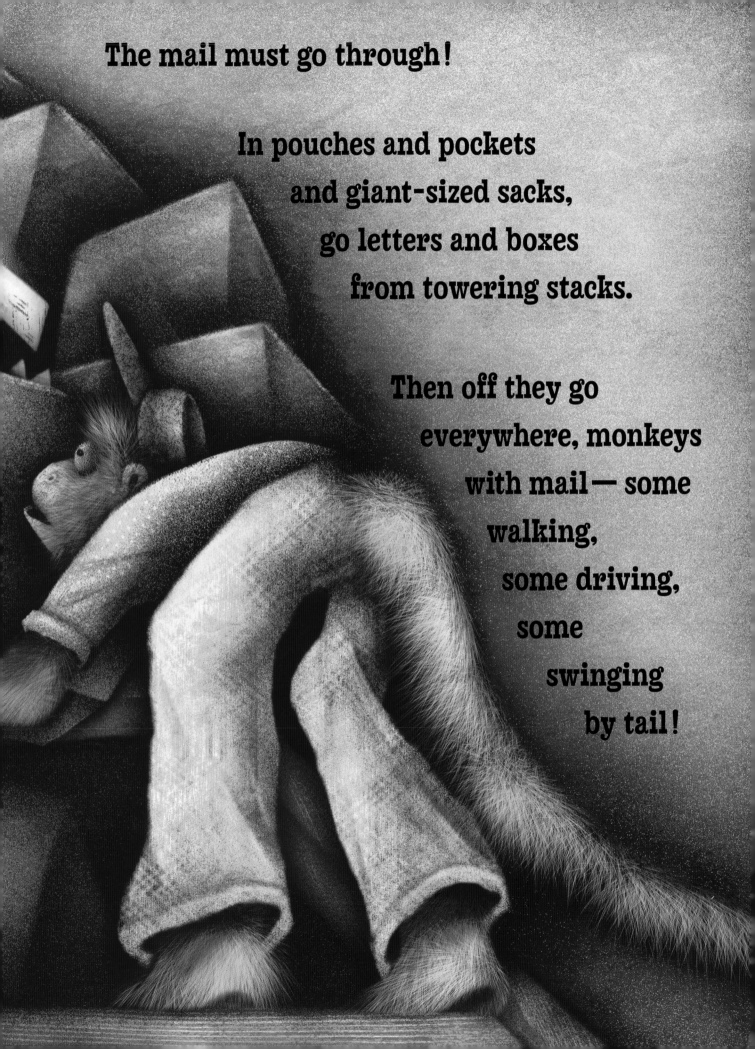

The mail must go through!

In pouches and pockets
and giant-sized sacks,
go letters and boxes
from towering stacks.

Then off they go
everywhere, monkeys
with mail— some
walking,
some driving,
some
swinging
by tail!

When stormy clouds gather
and rain drizzles down,
do monkeys complain?
Do they fret? Do they frown?

No! Because monkeys
know just what to do.
Their motto is always—

The mail must go through!

Sometimes their truck will get stuck in the muck when delivering letters to Bullfrog and Duck.

But storms never stop them.
They p-u-u-sh...
p-u-u-ll...and so...
their truck gets unstuck
and those monkeys can go!

But what if the mail has a
deep-sea address?

They pl-pl-plunge
in the ocean,
dive deep in the sea,
delivering packages
stamped C.O.D.
to Octopus, Dolphin,
Sea Turtle, and Whale
who thank those nice
monkeys for bringing
their mail!

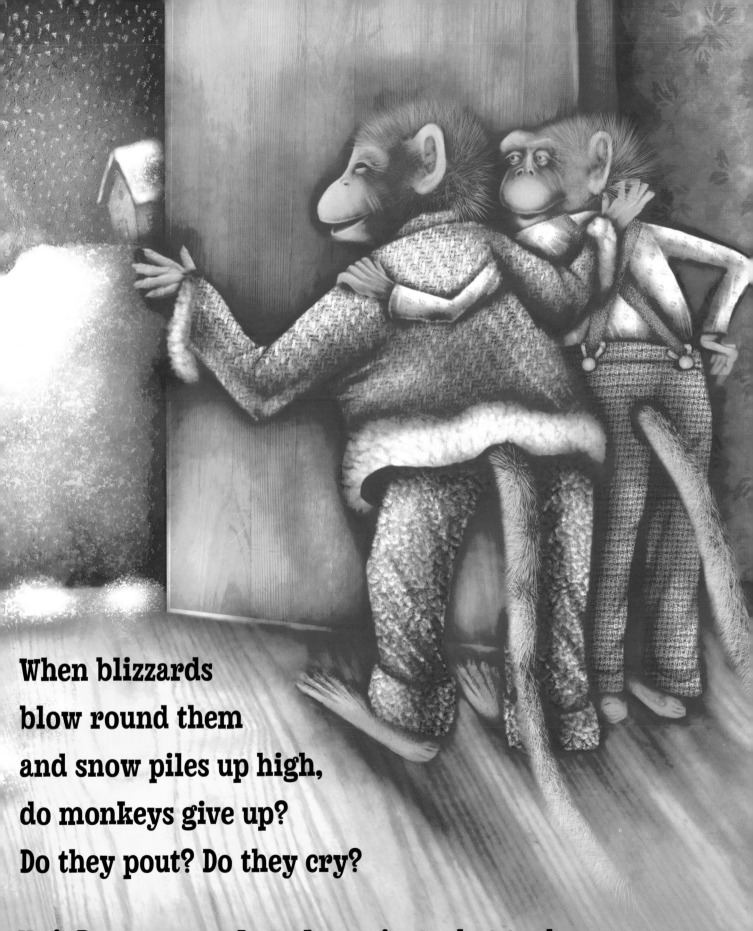

When blizzards
blow round them
and snow piles up high,
do monkeys give up?
Do they pout? Do they cry?

No! Because monkeys know just what to do.
Their motto is always—

The mail must go through!

They pull on warm mittens and long underwear, then stop at the mailbox of—brrrr!—Polar Bear.

They hop in their snow boots and fast snowmobile, rushing deliveries to Walrus and Seal.

But what if the mail is sent out of this world?

They bl-bl-blast off in rockets
and z-z-zoom up to space when letters
are sent to a far, outer place.

They z-z-zip through the darkness
past comets and stars, stopping at
Pluto, Uranus, and Mars.

When temperatures soar
in the jungle so hot,
do monkeys all mope?
Do they grumble a lot?

No! Because monkeys
know just what to do.
Their motto is always—

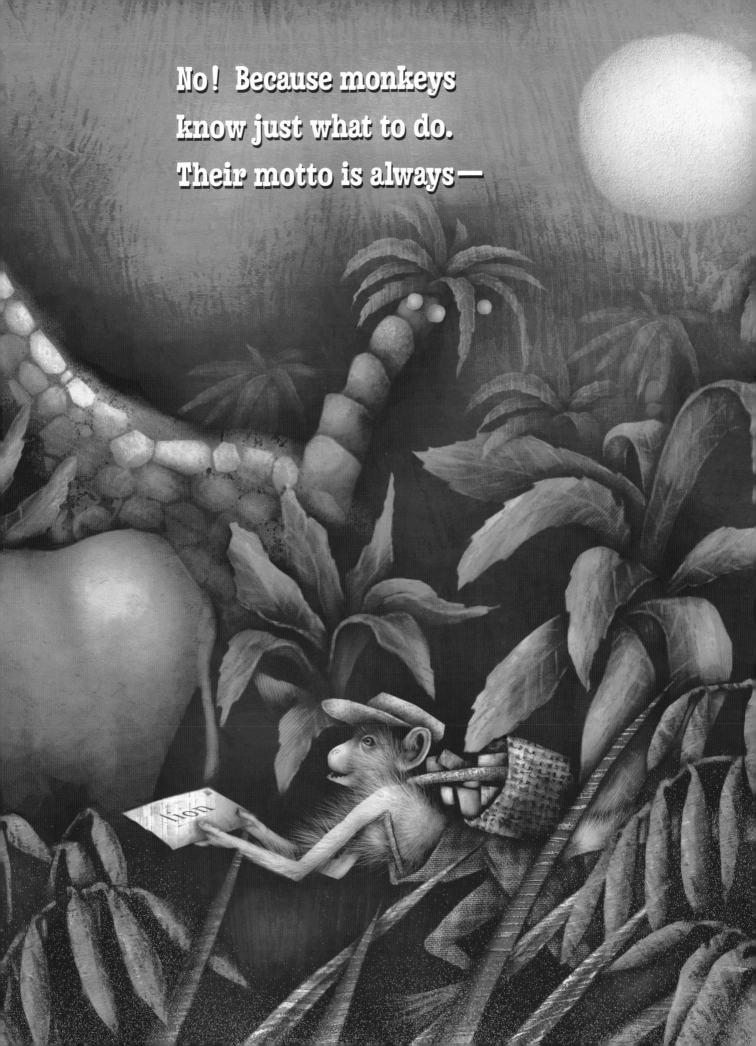

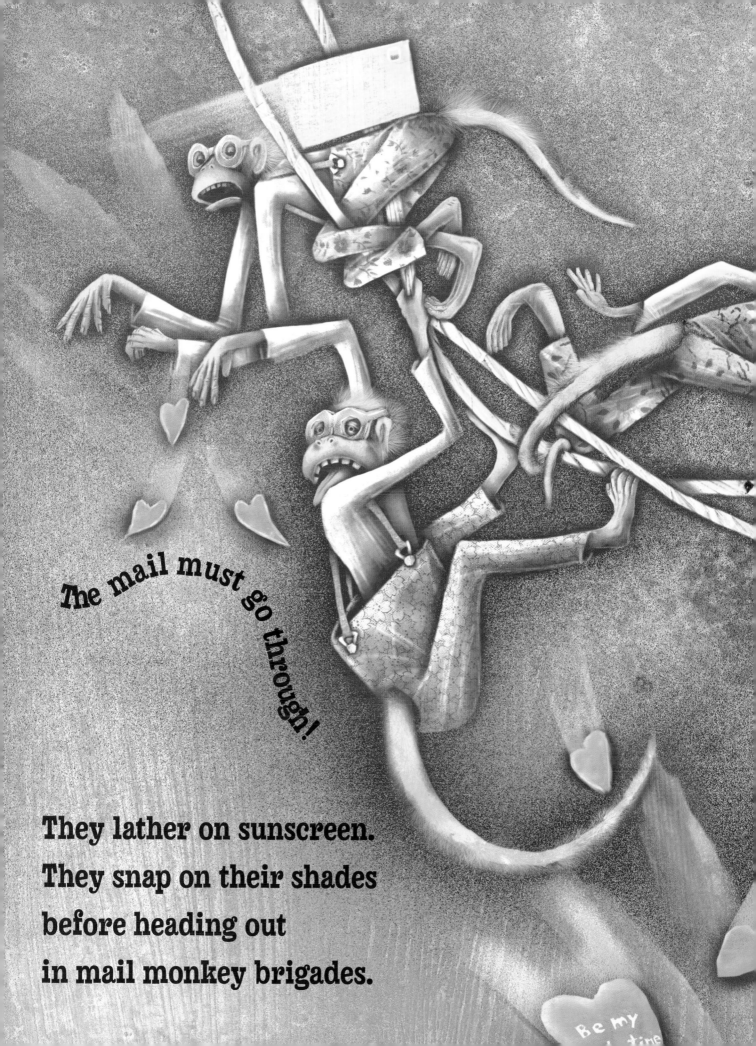

The mail must go through!

They lather on sunscreen.
They snap on their shades
before heading out
in mail monkey brigades.

They swing through the branches
on long, twisty vines,
passing out postcards
and pink valentines.

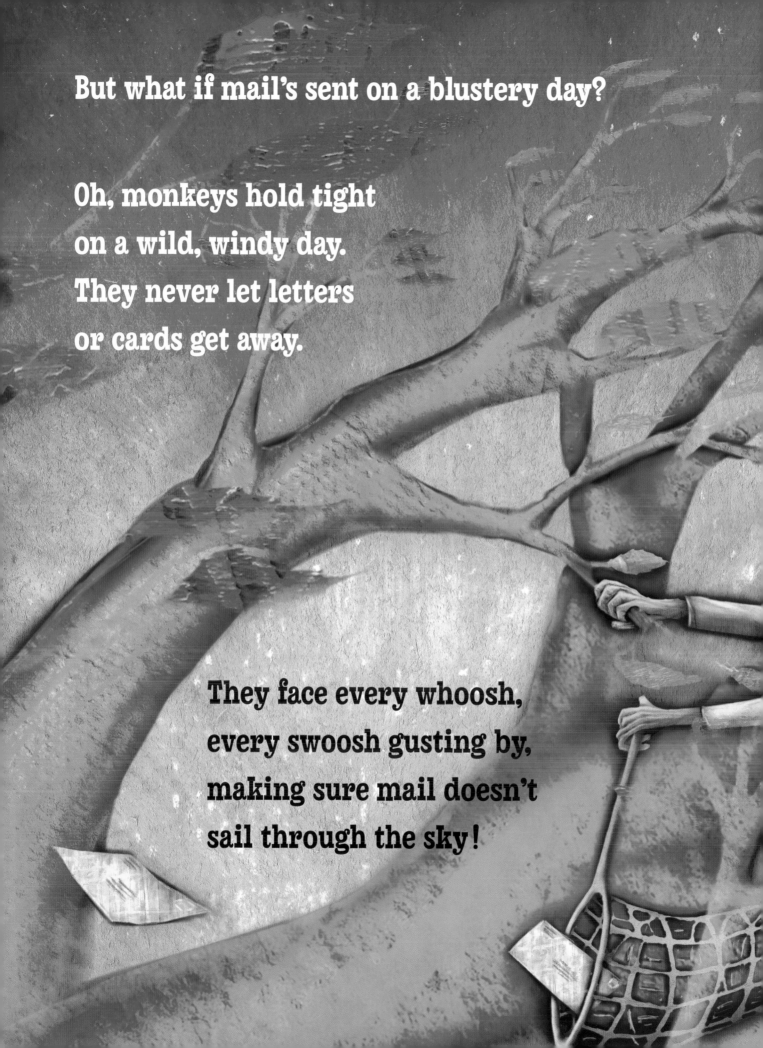

But what if mail's sent on a blustery day?

Oh, monkeys hold tight
on a wild, windy day.
They never let letters
or cards get away.

They face every whoosh,
every swoosh gusting by,
making sure mail doesn't
sail through the sky!

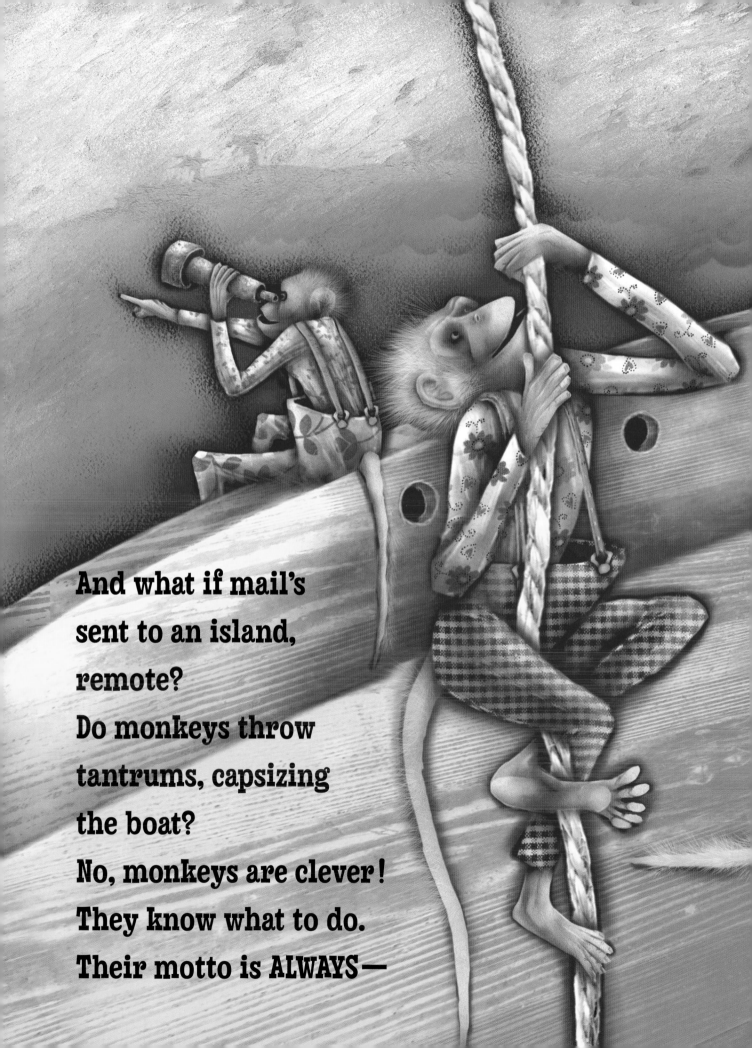

And what if mail's
sent to an island,
remote?
Do monkeys throw
tantrums, capsizing
the boat?
No, monkeys are clever!
They know what to do.
Their motto is ALWAYS—

The mail must go through!

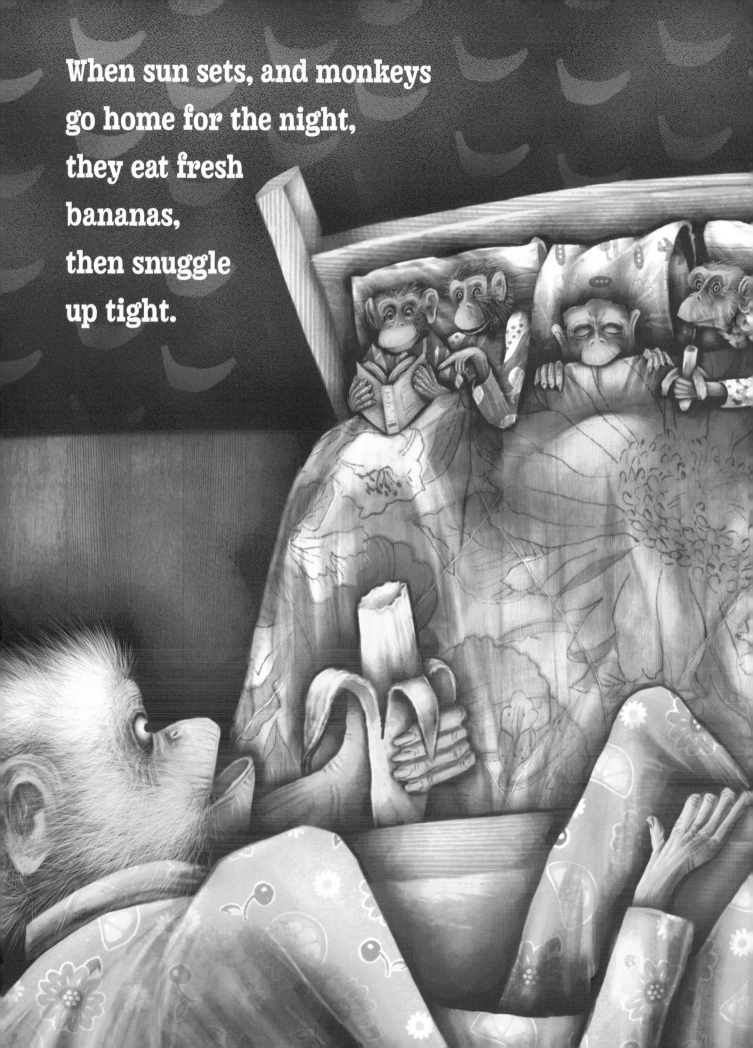

When sun sets, and monkeys
go home for the night,
they eat fresh
bananas,
then snuggle
up tight.

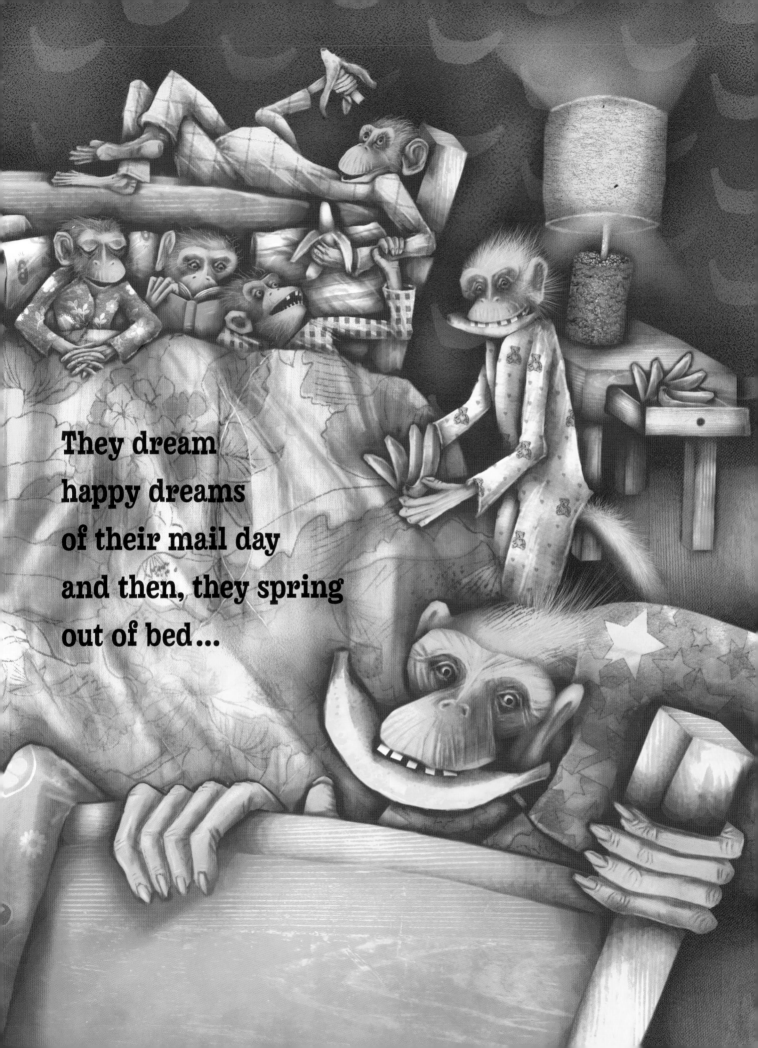

They dream
happy dreams
of their mail day
and then, they spring
out of bed...

to start over again !